SHOO, FLY GUY!

Tedd Arnold

Cartwheel
·B·O·O·K·S·®

SCHOLASTIC INC.

New York   Toronto   London   Auckland   Sydney
Mexico City   New Delhi   Hong Kong   Buenos Aires

Specially for Zachary Chase
—T. A.

ISBN-13: 978-0-545-07882-5
ISBN-10: 0-545-07882-2

Copyright © 2006 by Tedd Arnold. All rights reserved.
Published by Scholastic Inc. SCHOLASTIC,
CARTWHEEL BOOKS, and associated logos are trademarks
and/or registered trademarks of Scholastic Inc.

15 16/0

Printed in the U.S.A.   40

This edition first printing, March 2008

Chapter 1

A boy had a pet fly.
The boy called his pet Fly Guy.
Fly Guy could say the boy's

name—

BUZZ!

Buzz played with Fly Guy.

Buzz made him a glass house.

Best of all, Buzz fed him.

Fly Guy's favorite food was brown, oozy, lumpy, and smelly.

One day Fly Guy went
flying by himself.

When he came home,
Buzz was gone.

Fly Guy was hungry.
So off he flew.

Chapter 2

Fly Guy flew until he saw something to eat.

It wasn't oozy, lumpy, or smelly. But it was brown. Close enough!

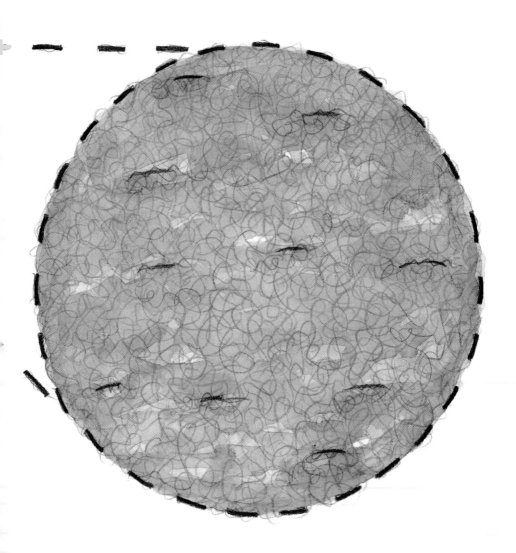

A boy shouted,
"That is my hamburger!"

"Shoo, fly!"

Fly Guy flew on until he
saw something else.

It wasn't brown, lumpy, or smelly. But it was oozy. Close enough!

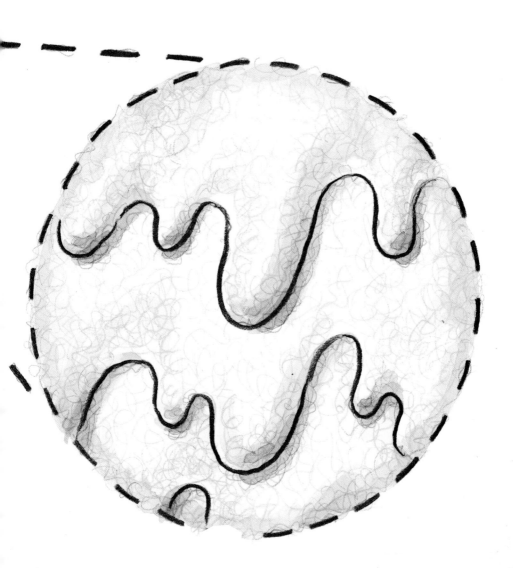

A girl yelled,
"That is my pizza!"

"Shoo, fly!"

Fly Guy flew on until
he saw something else.

It wasn't brown, oozy, or smelly. But it was lumpy. Close enough!

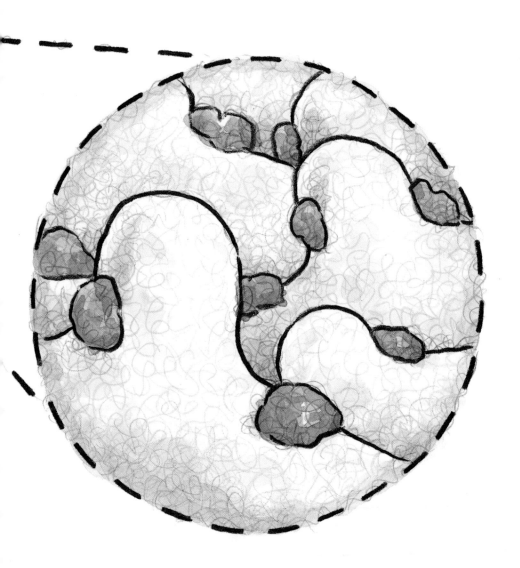

A dog growled,
"Those are my bones."

"Shoo, fly!"

Fly Guy flew on until he
saw something else.

It wasn't brown, oozy, or lumpy. But it was smelly. Close enough!

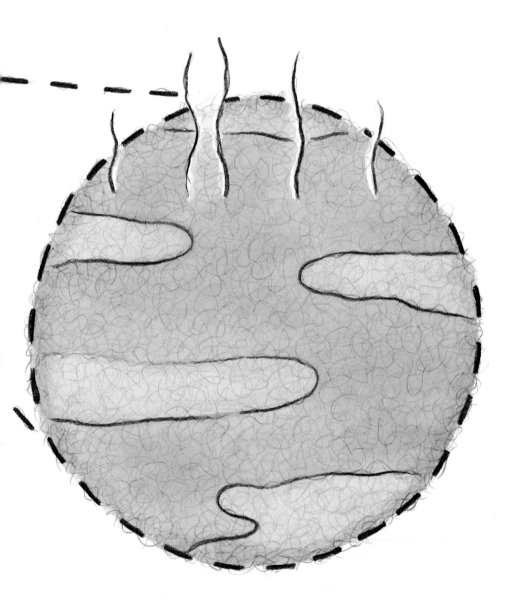

A bird squawked,
"That is my roadkill."

"Shoo, fly!"

Chapter 3

Fly Guy was very hungry.
And he was very tired.
He looked around.
Fly Guy was very lost.

He flew on and on and on and

and on until...

Fly Guy saw something.
Could it be? Yes!

It was brown, oozy,
lumpy, and smelly.

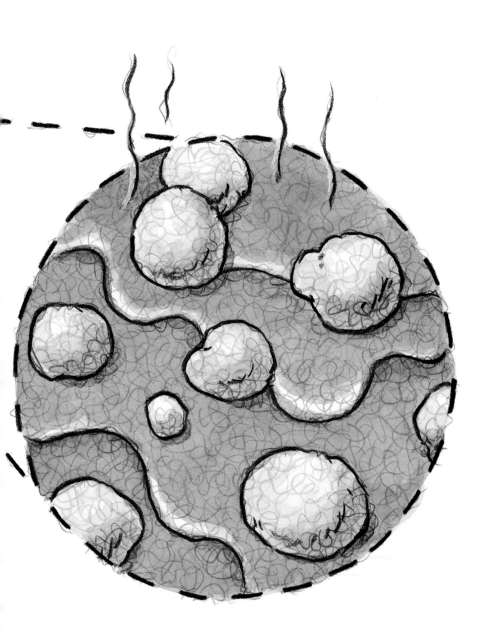

"You found our picnic!"
cried Buzz. "And here is
your favorite—Shoo Fly Pie!"
Fly Guy was very happy!